The
Tiara
Club
at Silver
Towers

For darling Annie, and the Princesses
Sophie and Izzy
x VF

For Lucy, a friend forever
x SG

www.tiaraclub.co.uk

First published by Orchard Books in 2006

ORCHARD BOOKS
338 Euston Road, London NW1 3BH
Orchard Books Australia
Hachette Children's Books
Level 17/207 Kent St, Sydney NSW 2000

A Paperback Original

Text © Vivian French 2006
Cover illustration © Sarah Gibb 2006

The right of Vivian French to be
identified as the author of this work
has been asserted by her in accordance with
the Copyright, Designs and Patents Act, 1988.

A CIP catalogue record for this book is available
from the British Library.

ISBN 1 84616 199 1

1 3 5 7 9 10 8 6 4 2

Orchard Books is a division of Hachette Children's Books

The Tiara Club
at Silver Towers

Princess Sophia
and the Prince's Party
By Vivian French

ORCHARD BOOKS

The Royal Palace Academy
for the *Preparation* of *Perfect Princesses*

(Known to our students as "*The Princess Academy*")

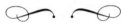

OUR SCHOOL MOTTO:
*A Perfect Princess always thinks of others
before herself, and is kind, caring and truthful.*

Silver Towers offers a complete education for
Tiara Club princesses with emphasis on selected
outings. The curriculum includes:

Fans and Curtseys	*Problem Prime Ministers*
A visit to Witch Windlespin	*A visit to the Museum of Royal Life*
(Royal herbalist, healer and maker of magic potions)	*(Students will be well protected from the Poisoned Apple)*

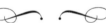

Our headteacher, Queen Samantha Joy, is present
at all times, and students are well looked after
by the school Fairy Godmother, Fairy Angora.

Our resident staff and visiting experts include:

LADY ALBINA MacSPLINTER (School Secretary)	*QUEEN MOTHER MATILDA (Etiquette, Posture and Poise)*
CROWN PRINCE DANDINO (School Excursions)	*FAIRY G (Head Fairy Godmother)*

We award tiara points to encourage our Tiara Club princesses towards the next level. All princesses who win enough points at Silver Towers will attend the Silver Ball, where they will be presented with their Silver Sashes.

Silver Sash Tiara Club princesses are invited to return to Ruby Mansions, our exclusive residence for Perfect Princesses, where they may continue their education at a higher level.

PLEASE NOTE:
Princesses are expected to arrive at the Academy with a *minimum* of:

TWENTY BALL GOWNS
(with all necessary hoops,
petticoats, etc)

TWELVE DAY DRESSES

SEVEN GOWNS
suitable for garden parties,
and other special
day occasions

TWELVE TIARAS

DANCING SHOES
five pairs

VELVET SLIPPERS
three pairs

RIDING BOOTS
two pairs

Cloaks, muffs, stoles, gloves
and other essential
accessories as required

Hello! I'm Princess Sophia,
and I'm a Tiara Club princess
here at Silver Towers - just like you!
And I'm SO glad you're here with us.
I expect you know my friends who share
Silver Rose Room with me. There's Alice,
and Daisy, and Katie and Charlotte and
Emily - and I just KNOW that if we
get enough Tiara Points to win our
Silver Sashes, and go on to Ruby Towers,
we'll still be the very best friends ever.
We're not too friendly with Princess
Diamonde and her twin sister Gruella,
though. They just LOVE showing off,
and being mean...

Chapter One

It was Wednesday, and we were late getting up. Katie was still in her pyjamas and Alice was only half-dressed when the last bell rang for breakfast. Charlotte dropped her hairbrush, and looked horrified.

"Oh NO!" she said. "Lady Albina's going to be FURIOUS!

We'll get about a million minus tiara points!"

Lady Albina is the school secretary, and she's usually floating about at breakfast time. She only smiles when Queen Samantha Joy is around, and she's always telling us off for not being Perfect Princesses – and handing out minus tiara points.

Emily groaned. "I've already got three this week," she said. "I forgot to hand in my Ideal Banquet Arrangements to Lady Victoria, and she was in a bad mood."

"But we did get five points each for knowing how to flutter a fan while curtseying," I said.

11

"You mean YOU did," Katie said as she scrambled into her dress. "I only got two."

Daisy sighed. "And me."

"Never mind about fans," Charlotte interrupted. "Just let's GO!"

We hurried down the stairs, hoping we might be able to sneak in without being seen...

But Lady Albina was standing outside the dining hall pinning a notice on the board. She frowned at us as we sank into our most apologetic curtsies.

"I'm SO sorry we're late, Lady Albina," I said.

Lady Albina looked at her watch in a meaningful way. "You are VERY LATE INDEED, Princess Sophia," she snapped. "Such behaviour is intolerable! Please report to Queen Samantha Joy immediately after breakfast, and I will not be at all surprised if she forbids you to attend Prince Maurice's party!" Then she sniffed loudy, and stalked away with her nose in the air.

We stared at each other. Finally Emily said, "Who's Prince Maurice? And why would he ask us to his party?"

Alice shook her head. "I don't

know. My big sister's never said anything about a Prince Maurice."

Charlotte sighed. "I do hope we can go. It's AGES since we've been to a party."

Daisy was looking worried. "Do you think Queen Samantha Joy will be VERY angry with us?"

"We'd better have breakfast and find out," Katie said, and we followed her into the dining hall.

Of course the only places left were next to the terrible twins, Diamonde and Gruella, and Diamonde looked SO superior as we sat down.

"Don't any of you know that

Perfect Princesses are meant to be on time for their appointments?" she asked.

We ignored her, and Emily turned to Gruella. "Do you know anything about a party?" she asked. "Prince Maurice's party?"

Gruella shook her head, but Diamonde snorted.

"Typical," she sneered. "Trust one of the Silver Rose Roomers to pretend she knows something before the rest of us!"

Emily went very pink, and bit her lip. I jumped up and glared at Diamonde.

"That's SO unfair!" I said. "Lady Albina told us!" As I spoke, I suddenly remembered. Lady Albina had been pinning up a notice when we saw her. I was so sure it was about the party that I went to check...and walked straight into our headteacher, Queen Samantha Joy.

Chapter Two

Queen Samantha Joy gave me an astonished stare.

"Would you mind telling me why you're not in the dining hall, Princess Sophia?" she asked.

"PLEASE forgive me, Your Majesty," I stammered, and I curtsied right down to the ground. "I was...I was going to look at the notice board."

Our headteacher turned to the board, and inspected it. "There is nothing here to attract such enthusiastic interest," she told me. "Only a note to say that from now on any princess who is late for breakfast will be given five minus tiara points. I trust, Princess Sophia, that YOU were not late this morning?"

I didn't know what to say. I hung my head, and stared at the floor. "Yes, Your Majesty," I whispered. "Lady Albina said we were to report to you after breakfast."

Queen Samantha Joy frowned.

"This is NOT the way I expect my princesses to behave," she said. "Do YOU think it is the way to behave, Princess Sophia?"

My eyes filled with tears.

The one thing I've always wanted more than anything else in the whole wide world is to be a Perfect Princess – and I'd TOTALLY let myself down. All I could think of to say was, "I'm so very VERY sorry, Your Majesty."

"So I should hope," the headteacher said. "And now, you'd better come with me. I have an announcement to make."

She swept into the dining hall, and I hurried after her.

I could see my friends looking anxious as I slid into my

seat, but I couldn't tell them
what had happened because
Queen Samantha Joy was
already speaking.

"Princesses! My nephew, Prince Maurice of Charmover, has graduated from the Royal Academy for the Preparation of Perfect Princes with nine hundred and ninety-five crown points out of a possible one thousand. The Academy would like to celebrate his remarkable achievement, and

the headteacher, King Ferdinand, has invited every one of you to a ball to be held at the Princes' Academy next Saturday evening. Queen Samantha Joy stopped, and smiled. "And I've arranged for extra dancing lessons, so the princesses from Silver Towers will be the belles of the ball!"

It was so quiet you could have heard a pin drop. Truly! And then EVERYBODY began to talk at once, until our headteacher raised her hand.

"I'm glad you're pleased," she said. "Of course, it goes without saying that I expect only the BEST behaviour from my girls!

Which reminds me..." She turned, and looked sternly at me. "Princess Sophia, tell me truthfully. Do you think you deserve to go to Prince Maurice's party?"

I didn't know what to say. I felt AWFUL! Of course I was absolutely DYING to go – but I wanted to win my Silver Sash and go on to Ruby Mansions even more. I took a deep breath, and curtsied again.

"Your Majesty," I said, "I'm very, very sorry. And I don't know if I deserve to go to the party." I swallowed hard. "But whatever you decide, I do promise to try to behave better in future."

Queen Samantha Joy looked thoughtful, but before she could say anything Emily stood up.

"Please, Your Majesty," she said, "if Sophia can't go, then I oughtn't to go either."

"Nor me," Alice said, and she, Charlotte, Katie and Daisy stood up as well.

"We were ALL late for breakfast, Your Majesty," Katie explained.

"I see!" Queen Samantha Joy gave a little chuckle. "Well, perhaps Princess Sophia SHOULD go to the party. Any princess who inspires such loyalty in her friends must be worthy of a second chance!"

"THANK YOU, Your Majesty," I said. "Oh – THANK YOU!"

Our headteacher nodded at me. "Just remember, Princess Sophia – no third chances!" And she swept away.

I sank into my chair. "Thank you all SO much," I said to my friends. "That was SO lovely of you!"

"But we couldn't have gone without you," Emily said.

"Silver Rose Roomers for ever!" Katie cheered.

Diamonde sniffed. "Well," she said, "if Queen Samantha Joy had asked ME, I'd have said none of you deserved to go!" And she flounced out of the dining hall.

Alice grinned. "Never mind her – What are we going to WEAR?"

Chapter Three

We were still trying to decide when the five-minute warning bell went for first lesson. We hurried off to our Wednesday tutorial on Problem Prime Ministers, but halfway up the stairs we met Princess Eglantine coming down with Princess Nancy.

"All tutorials are cancelled,"

she said happily. "We've got
dancing instead – we've got to
go to the Silver Ballroom."

"Hurrah!" Charlotte did
a pirouette on the stair. "PPM is
SO boring. Who's taking the
dancing lessons?"

Freya grinned. "We think it might be Fairy Angora – but we're not sure."

"Oh – DOUBLE hurrah!" Alice said, and we all positively bounced back down the stairs and made our way to the ballroom. Fairy Angora is our school Fairy Godmother, and she's just WONDERFUL...even if she's a bit scatty at times.

But it wasn't Fairy Angora waiting for us. It was Lady Albina, and my heart sank as I saw her. I had this horrible feeling that I was CERTAIN to get into trouble again – and I'd end up not being allowed to go to Prince Maurice's party.

Lady Albina gave me SUCH a frosty look when she saw me, but she didn't say anything. She sailed across the room, and signalled to the Silver Towers musicians. They began to play a really skippy sort of tune; it made my feet twitch just hearing it!

Lady Albina frowned at them. "Stop that at once!' she ordered, and she sounded SO rude. "We need something MUCH slower!"

I saw the conductor give the

musicians the teeniest of winks, and they began to play the gloomiest music ever. DAH... DAH...DAH...it went.

It was SO hard not to laugh. I had to pretend I was blowing my nose, because I knew that if I did laugh, Lady Albina would be FURIOUS. Alice, Emily and Katie turned their giggles into coughs, but Daisy and Charlotte didn't manage nearly so well.

"Princess Daisy! Princess Charlotte! I do NOT see anything to laugh about!" Lady Albina snapped. "Please TRY and behave properly!"

"Yes, Lady Albina," Charlotte said, and Daisy curtsied.

"H'mph!" Lady Albina glared at the musicians. "Please play faster!"

The musicians burst into a wonderfully catchy polka, and

at once every princess seized a partner, and began to bound around the room.

"No no no NO!" Lady Albina clapped her hands to stop us. "You have been invited to the Princes' Academy, and this ridiculous hopping and skipping is MOST unsuitable. You must sit calmly until a prince invites you to dance, and then you will either waltz or foxtrot as appropriate. Princess Daisy, please come here. You too, Princess Sophia. I will teach you the basic steps, and I expect EVERYONE to pay close attention. Musicians – a slow tempo waltz, IF you please!"

The next hour was AWFUL! Lady Albina made me dance the boy's steps, so I was going forwards, while Daisy did the girl's steps, so she was going backwards. Lady

Albina kept saying, "One two THREE one two THREE!" when I absolutely knew the music was going ONE two three, ONE two three, and every single princess was getting more and more muddled. They were trying to copy what Lady Albina told

Daisy and me to do, but as we kept getting it wrong they did too. It was truly terrible! Lady Albina got crosser and crosser, and her instructions made less and less sense. I thought she was going to explode as I trod on poor Daisy's toes for about the millionth time, but luckily the bell went for the end of the lesson, and she stormed out.

We felt really gloomy as we trailed out of the ballroom. We'd always absolutely loved dancing before, but somehow Lady Albina made it seem so difficult. And it didn't get much better on Thursday or Friday.

"I think my feet are getting bigger," I sighed as we were dismissed from our last lesson.

"It was't QUITE so bad today," Charlotte said. "And it honestly isn't your fault – Lady Albina's

completely hopeless at telling us what to do."

Gruella sniggered. "Lady Albina said you made elephants look graceful."

"Never mind her." Alice put her arm through mine. "Let's go and try on our dresses for tomorrow."

Chapter Four

Can you keep a secret?

Yes. I know you can.

I really REALLY hate being bad at things. Is that dreadful of me? But it's true.

I woke up really early on the morning of Prince Maurice's party because I was SO worried. I don't want to boast, but I'd

always been much the best
at dancing in Fairy Angora's
classes – but Lady Albina had
made me feel as if I could never
dance again. I looked across at
my gorgeous ballgown and my
shoes and my fan, and instead of
feeling excited I felt sick.

"Sophia? Are you OK?" Daisy was sitting up in bed.

"I think so," I said.

Alice yawned. "It'll be fun to see the Princes' Academy," she said. "What do you think the princes will be like?"

"Most boys are boring." Emily was awake too. "My brothers certainly are."

"Diamonde thinks Prince Maurice will sweep her off her feet and dance with her until midnight," Charlotte said with a giggle. "But Gruella thinks he'll choose her – I heard them arguing about it!"

Katie threw back her covers. "He must be really old," she pointed out. "He won't take any notice of any of us. Come on – let's get up!"

By the time the coaches came to collect us I was feeling a bit better.

After all, I had all my lovely friends, even if my dancing was hopeless. And it WAS nice to have a chance to wear my very best ballgown.

As the coach drew up at the front door of the Princes' Academy Katie gave a thumbs up. It wasn't a very princessy thing to do, but it made us giggle.

The princes' ballroom was WONDERFUL! The walls were a fabulous red, and the ceiling was glittering gold. There were masses of sparkling chandeliers, and down one side of the room was a row of golden pillars. Behind them I could see tables piled with food, and lots of comfy sofas, but the ballroom seemed very empty – at one end a group of princes was huddled together looking awkward, and at the other, a row of princesses was sitting stiffly on little golden chairs.

"Oops!" Alice whispered in my ear. "It doesn't look much fun!"

We made our way to the chairs, and sat down.

"Maybe we'll sit here all evening," Emily said, but at that moment there was a fanfare of trumpets. A large king dressed in the most splendid robes came marching in, and beside him was Queen Samantha Joy looking MAGNIFICENT.

"No one dancing? T'CHAH! Can't have that!" the king boomed. "Start the music! Everyone dance! Come along, boys! Lots of pretty princesses here! Choose a partner, and off you go!"

At once the musicians burst into a waltz.

None of the princes moved.

"Come along!" the king barked at them. "This is a BALL! You're meant to DANCE!"

The princes shifted about, and at last a tall, very handsome prince walked towards us.

"Bet that's Prince Maurice," Charlotte said. "Look at Diamonde and Gruella!"

Diamonde and Gruella were both sitting bolt upright, fluttering their fans madly, and smiling absolutely HUGE

smiles – but the prince took no notice of them. He came straight towards me, and bowed.

"May I have the honour of this dance, Your Highness?" he asked.

I stood up, and the prince grabbed my hand and swung me onto the floor – and I was waltzing.

Only I wasn't, because everything Lady Albina had said suddenly flooded into my head, and my feet felt HUGE. Instead of dancing backwards I stepped forwards. At once I knew that was SO wrong, so I tried to change, trod on my own toes, wobbled, staggered – and fell over!

Chapter Five

I don't think I've ever EVER been so embarrassed! My face was burning red as I struggled to my feet, and I RAN. Behind me I heard the tall prince absolutely howling with laughter, and I just wanted to die. I dashed between the pillars, and hid behind a sofa in a corner. I shut my eyes and flapped my fan to cool my face, and thought, "I mustn't cry! I mustn't cry! Perfect Princesses don't feel sorry for themselves..." but it was SO hard.

And then I heard a noise. A tiny cough.

I opened my eyes, and peeped over the arm of the sofa. A very ordinary looking prince with tufty hair was standing on the other side holding a glass of water and a white hankie. When he saw me looking he bowed, very politely.

"It's quite all right to cry, you know," he said, and he smiled the sweetest smile. "It's horrible when people laugh at you. People often laugh at me, and I never quite get used to it. Would you like the hankie? Or would you prefer the water?"

I couldn't help staring at him. He was about my height, so I thought

he must be quite young. He wasn't at all like I'd expected a prince to be, but he was so kind I couldn't help smiling back.

"The water, please," I said.

"Good choice," the prince said. "I knew as soon as I saw you that you were a Perfect Princess."

I shook my head. "Prince Maurice doesn't think so," I said.

A strange expression flitted across the tufty-haired prince's face. "Prince Maurice?" he asked.

"He asked me to dance, and I fell over," I explained. "He couldn't stop laughing!"

"Oh – yes. Yes, I saw that," the prince said, and he hesitated. "Don't you think that was rather mean of him?"

"Erm...I suppose it was," I said slowly. "But I don't know

anything about princes and how they should behave."

The prince shook his head. "No Perfect Prince should EVER laugh at the misfortunes of others!" Although they laughed at me all the time in dancing lessons. They made me dance the girl's steps, you see, because I'm small," he sighed. "That's why I'm hiding here. I got five minus crown points, and I don't dare ask anyone to dance."

I began to giggle. "But that's what happened to ME!" I said. "Only the other way round, of course." And then an AMAZING idea popped into my head, and before I could stop myself I said, "Why don't we dance together? It won't matter a bit if we get it wrong – we're both used to it!"

The tufty haired prince's eyes shone, and he smiled a HUGE smile.

"Would you really dance with me?" he asked.

"Of course!" I said, and at that exact moment the musicians burst into the hoppiest skippiest polka you've ever heard. "Come on!" I said, and we absolutely zoomed onto the

dance floor. Round and round we danced, and as we passed my friends Katie seized Charlotte, and Emily caught Daisy's hand and they whizzed after us...and then I saw Alice twirling round and round with a prince! It was SUCH fun...

And then the music stopped, and there was the LOUDEST cheer. It was SO loud it made the chandeliers shake! And I suddenly realised – *the cheer was for me and the tufty-haired prince!*

Queen Samantha Joy sailed onto the dance floor, and her eyes were twinkling.

"I wish to extend my congratulations to Princess Sophia, the first princess ever to persuade my beloved nephew, Prince Maurice, to dance!"

I stared at the tufty-haired prince. HE was Prince Maurice!

"And very fine dancers they

both are!" the king agreed as he strode up. "So fine, indeed, that I have to award Prince Maurice his last five crown points – so he now has ONE THOUSAND!"

And everybody burst into more wild cheering...until Prince Maurice stepped forward.

"I'd just like to say," he said, "that the only reason I'm dancing is because I've found the Perfect Princess to dance with!" He turned to me, and bowed – and as he stood up he winked SUCH a cheerful wink. "And now I've found my dancing feet I shall ask Princess Sophia to be my partner in the Princes' Academy Celebration Waltz!"

Chapter Six

The rest of the evening was SO fabulous. We Rose Roomers danced with each other, and we danced with the princes, and once I even danced with the king! Luckily it was a country dance, so I didn't have to worry about going forwards or backwards...

And when the time came to go home we collapsed into the coach feeling SO happy.

Just as the coachman was about to shake his reins the coach door opened, and Queen Samantha Joy smiled in at us.

"I wanted to say how proud I am of you, my dears," she said. She

leant across and took my hand. "You did SO well, Princess Sophia. Prince Maurice was quite right. You are indeed a Perfect Princess, and you and your friends from Silver Rose Room truly deserve to be the belles of the ball!" Then she blew us a kiss, and closed the coach door.

That night I dreamed wonderful dreams of floating in a silver ballroom with all my friends ...

And I just KNOW you were there too.

What happens next?
Find out in

Princess Emily
and the Wishing Star

Hi! This is Princess Emily
saying hello and I'm SO pleased
you're here with us at Silver Towers.
Charlotte, Katie, Daisy, Alice, Sophia
and I have SUCH a good time...except
when horrid Princess Diamonde
and her twin sister, Gruella,
try and spoil everything, of course.
We'd been keeping our fingers crossed
for ages that we'd got enough tiara points
to win our Silver Sashes, but suddenly
it was nearly time for the Silver Ball.
And we began to panic – especially me!

Check out

The Tiara Club

website at:

www.tiaraclub.co.uk

You"ll find Perfect Princess games and fun things to do, as well as news on the Tiara Club and all your favourite princesses!

The
Tiara
Club

Win a Tiara Club
Perfect Princess Prize!

Look for the secret word in mirror writing hidden in a tiara in each of the Tiara Club books. Each book has one word. Put together the six words from books **7** to **12** to make a special Perfect Princess sentence, then send it to us together with 20 words or more on why you like the Tiara Club books. Each month, we will put the correct entries in a draw and one lucky reader will receive a magical Perfect Princess prize!

Send your Perfect Princess sentence, your name
and your address on a postcard to:
The Tiara Club Competition,
Orchard Books, 338 Euston Road,
London, NW1 3BH

Australian readers should write to:
Hachette Children's Books,
Level 17/207 Kent Street, Sydney, NSW 2000.

Only one entry per child.
Final draw: 31 August 2007

By Vivian French
Illustrated by Sarah Gibb

PRINCESS CHARLOTTE		
AND THE BIRTHDAY BALL	ISBN	1 84362 863 5
PRINCESS KATIE		
AND THE SILVER PONY	ISBN	1 84362 860 0
PRINCESS DAISY		
AND THE DAZZLING DRAGON	ISBN	1 84362 864 3
PRINCESS ALICE		
AND THE MAGICAL MIRROR	ISBN	1 84362 861 9
PRINCESS SOPHIA		
AND THE SPARKLING SURPRISE	ISBN	1 84362 862 7
PRINCESS EMILY		
AND THE BEAUTIFUL FAIRY	ISBN	1 84362 859 7

The Tiara Club at Silver Towers

PRINCESS CHARLOTTE		
AND THE ENCHANTED ROSE	ISBN	1 84616 195 9
PRINCESS KATIE		
AND THE DANCING BROOM	ISBN	1 84616 196 7
PRINCESS DAISY		
AND THE MAGICAL MERRY-GO-ROUND	ISBN	1 84616 197 5
PRINCESS ALICE		
AND THE CRYSTAL SLIPPER	ISBN	1 84616 198 3
PRINCESS SOPHIA		
AND THE PRINCE'S PARTY	ISBN	1 84616 199 1
PRINCESS EMILY		
AND THE WISHING STAR	ISBN	1 84616 200 9

All priced at £3.99.

The Tiara Club books are available from all good bookshops, or can be ordered direct
from the publisher: Orchard Books, PO BOX 29, Douglas IM99 1BQ.
Credit card orders please telephone 01624 836000 or fax 01624 837033 or visit our
Internet site: www.wattspub.co.uk or e-mail: bookshop@enterprise.net for details.

To order please quote title, author, ISBN and your full name and address.
Cheques and postal orders should be made payable to "Bookpost plc.©
Postage and packing is FREE within the UK
(overseas customers should add £2.00 per book).

Prices and availability are subject to change.